A story of passion, persever

My Violin is NOT Broken?

by Evelyn Grundy

Mintwood Press
Reston. VA
© 2022 Evelyn Grundy.

Names: Grundy. Evelyn. 1979- author. illustrator.
Title: My violin is NOT broken? / by Evelyn Grundy.
Description: [Reston. Virginia] : Mintwood Press. [2023] | "A story of passion. perseverance. and grit!" | Audience: Juvenile. |
Summary: A young girl wants to play the violin. but herviolin sounds terrible. It groans. shrieks. and whines. leaving her disappointed. frustrated. and downright annoyed. Will she ever be able to make her violin sing?--Publisher.
Identifiers: ISBN: 979-8-9871093-0-4 (paperback) | 979-8-9871093-1-1 (hardcover) | LCCN: 2022920866
Subjects: LCSH: Violin--Instruction and study--Juvenile fiction. | Girls--Juvenile fiction. | Perseverance (Ethics)--Juvenile fiction. | Disappointment--Juvenile fiction. | Sounds--Juvenile fiction. | CYAC: Violin--Instruction and study--Fiction. | Girls--Fiction. | Perseverance--Fiction. | Disappointment--Fiction. | Sound--Fiction.
Classification: LCC: PZ7.1.G7962 M9 2023 | DDC: [E]--dc23

Edited by Miriam Bulmer | Book Design by Arlene Soto

To my son, Cyrus, may your love of music, enthusiasm,
and creative mind charge into the world with unbridled passion.
This book is for you.

To all the struggling learners, I see you and I'm rooting for you.
This book is for you.

To anyone who has ever wanted to quit anything hard,
This book is for you.

And to my husband, Joe, whose patience got me through.

Cyrus, I wrote this story for you, but it turned out to be a story
about me. I guess we have some things in common after all.

When I was five, I met a girl with a violin.
She was standing to one side of the
farmers market, her violin case open at her
feet, playing a simple, magical tune.

"How do you do it?" I asked.
"With lots of practice," she smiled.

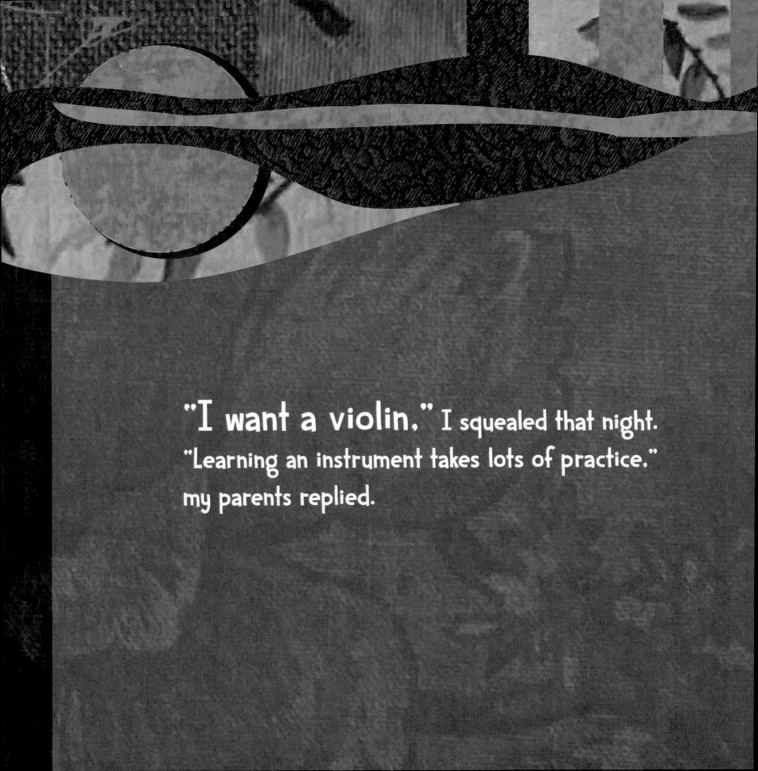

"I want a violin," I squealed that night. "Learning an instrument takes lots of practice," my parents replied.

I decided to **make** a violin.

My parents seemed impressed.

That summer, I got a **real violin.**
I clutched it tightly the entire way
home, eager to hear it sing.

I ran to my room, closed the door, and
cracked open the case. I held my violin
under my chin and pulled the bow across
the strings, just like the girl at the market.

My violin sounded

TERRIBLE!

For seven days, I practiced.
Each morning I tried again, pulling the
bow across the strings. My violin only
groaned, whined,
and shrieked in response.

"It's broken!" I yelled on Friday evening.
My parents laughed—"Learning an
instrument takes lots of ..."
"Practice," I mumbled.
Clearly, they hadn't been paying attention.

1 Sunday	
2 Monday	
3 Tuesday	
4 Wednesday	
5 Thursday	
6 Friday	
7 Saturday	

When the leaves turned red,
I met a teacher with a violin.
She taught me to bend at the waist
to take a bow and to hold my violin
under my chin with no hands.
She told me to practice just
that for a whole week!

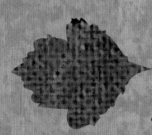

"But I want to play **all** the notes,"
I pleaded. "You will," she smiled.
"Learning an instrument takes
lots of practice."

By the time the snow fell. I could play the notes.
But my violin still would **not sing!** I practiced.

I practiced high. I practiced low. I practiced fast. even slow. My clumsy fingers landed in all the wrong places. My shoulders ached and I squirmed at the scratchy. not-so-right notes.

I huffed.

I grunted.

I cried.

Down, up, down, up went my bow. It wasn't pretty.

I moved my bow toward my fingers.

Too slippery.

I moved my bow toward the bridge.

Too scratchy.

I adjusted and adjusted.

My face turned red and I wanted to throw my useless,

no-good violin

away.

It was too hard.

I quit.

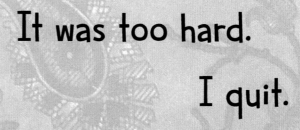

When the trees began to bud,

I found an idea.

Musicians wanted to play at the market.

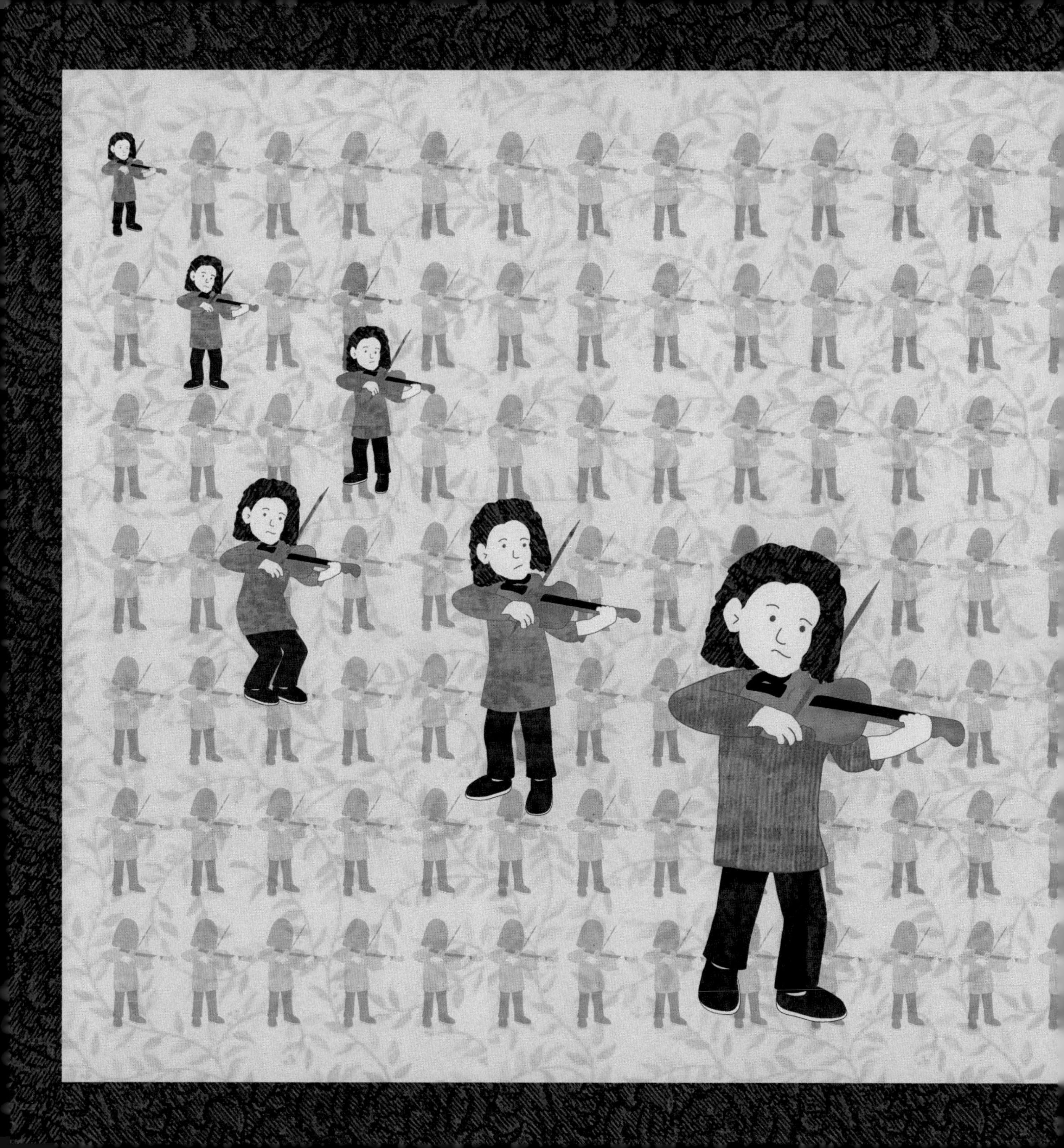

I wasn't sure I could do it, but I decided
to give my violin **one last try.**

My bow wobbled between the
fingerboard and the bridge as I played
for the ten-hundredth time.

I closed my eyes and remembered the girl at the market.

Suddenly my violin began to sing!

My head snapped upward, pulling my shoulders backward.

Floating through the air, music filled my room.

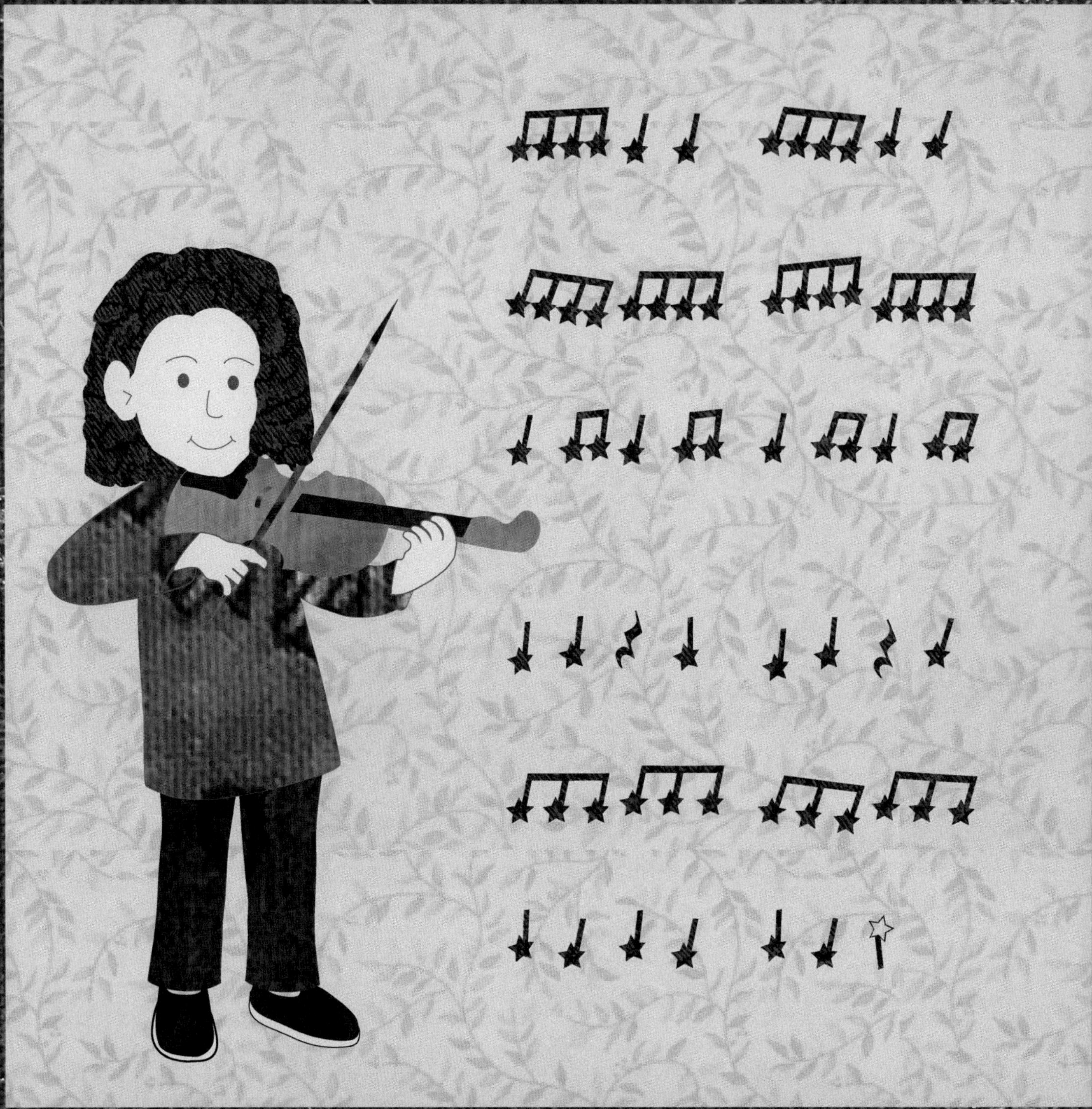

Confidence danced inside me
as I realized I could play "Twinkle, Twinkle"
six different ways.

When I was six, I met another girl with a violin. This time, I was the girl. I was standing to the side of the market, playing a simple tune, which sounded the best I knew it could.

"How do you do it?" a young boy asked.

"With lots and lots of practice,"
I beamed.

The story behind the illustrations

Years ago, my mother was given fabric squares by her longtime friend and asked to create a friendship square. Feeling stuck, she reached out to me, asking if I would be up for completing the project. I was delighted and created a few digital samples to choose from. And this was the final result!

This inspired the illustrations for this book.

Can I do it?

Exploring the book

Vocabulary

PERSEVERANCE: continued effort to do or achieve something despite difficulty or delay in achieving success.

GRIT: passion and perseverance toward a goal despite being confronted by significant obstacles and distractions.

PRACTICE: doing something regularly or repeatedly to improve your skill at doing it.

Discussion Questions

- What does the girl want to learn? Why?
- What's one thing you want to learn? Why?
- Was learning the violin what she expected? Why or why not?
- Was her violin broken? Why or why not?
- What did she do when she became frustrated?
- Did she like practicing her violin?
- Why did she keep practicing the violin?
- What's one thing you are learning that feels frustrating?
- What's one thing you can do when practicing feels hard?

About the Author and Illustrator

That's me!

Hi, I'm Evelyn Grundy. I have loved the violin ever since hearing a young busker at the NW Folklife Festival in Seattle. Practicing, however, was a completely different matter. Now, watching my son struggle through similar discomforts, I want to let young learners and their parents know it's okay to feel frustrated. Learning can be hard, and perseverance and grit are complex concepts. That's why this book was written.

Using my graphic design skills, I modeled the illustrations after a quilting project I completed years ago, giving the book a beautiful, unique feel that can be appreciated by all.

Learn more at www.violinpicturebook.com.

Made in the USA
Las Vegas, NV
16 November 2023

80811697R00024